Quest for God's Hidden Creatures:

Book Two

The Concealed Caverns

by Tom Bazow

SupernaturalArmor.com

The following is a work of fiction. The characters, circumstances and hidden worlds are products of the author's imagination. Any resemblances to persons living or dead is entirely coincidental.

Quest for God's Hidden Creatures:
The Concealed Caverns
© 2012 by Tom Bazow
Published in 2012 by Tom Bazow LLC

Contact the publisher SupernaturalArmor.com/contact/

ISBN: 978-0-9777725-3-7

Cover Design by Alane Pearce Professional Writing Services, LLC
Layout by Alane Pearce Professional Writing Services, LLC
Editing by Alane Pearce Professional Writing Services, LLC
Publishing

Publishing and Promotion Consulting by Alane Pearce Professional Writing Services, LLC and Author Coach.

AlanePearce.com or alane@AlanePearce.com

Interior artwork drawn by:
Kate Goodberlet age 10
Corbin Pearce age 11
Molly Goodberlet age 14

Author Photograph by Karon Root Photography, St. Louis MO
KaronRoot.com

        Quest for God's Hidden Creatures: The Concealed Caverns/
Tom Bazow
        1. Children's Books 2. Action/Adventure 3. Religious

It may have taken a few years for this sequel in the "Quest" series to be written, but it was well worth the wait. Along the way Tom has learned that when God gives someone a passion to write, time is never an obstacle. With faith and perseverance anything can be accomplished. Tom wishes to encourage everyone to follow their hearts and faithfully seek the Lord. And if you happen to encounter Zeke, the Tree Traveler, you just might want to listen.

Acknowledgements

My sincerest thanks go out to my beloved family for the support you give. Hannah and Molly, you two are awesome. Warrine without your belief in me I'm not sure this project would have been completed.

Thank you to the Goodberlet family. Thank you, Mike, for your support and endorsement. Amy, as always your suggestions were spot on. Molly and Kate, I am so grateful for your artistic talents.

A big thanks to my Publishing Consultant/Editor/Designer, Alane Pearce. Your expertise and encouragement made this book happen. A big thank you to Corbin Pearce for your wonderful illustrations.

And I have to thank Christian author, Michael Gunter for steering me to Alane.

Lastly, to all fans of Quest for God's Hidden Creatures: The Legacy of the Doors, I'm grateful. The fact that you asked, "When's the sequel gonna be published?" inspired me to move forward.

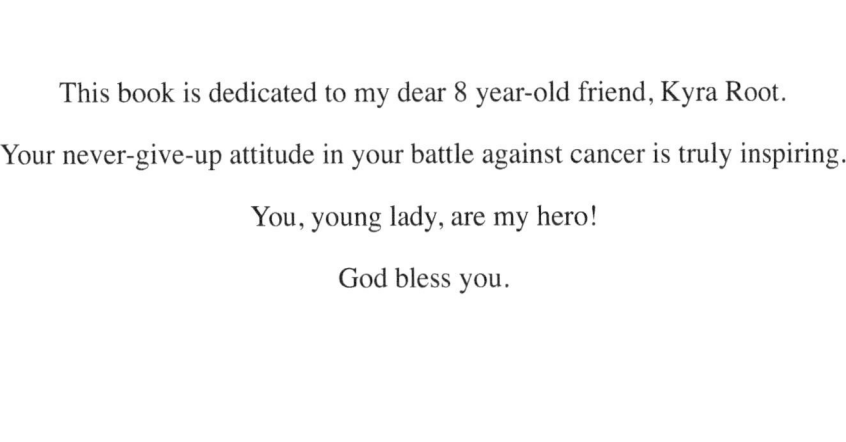

This book is dedicated to my dear 8 year-old friend, Kyra Root.

Your never-give-up attitude in your battle against cancer is truly inspiring.

You, young lady, are my hero!

God bless you.

The Mirror's Reflection

The school bus full of children flew down Interstate 44, seemingly out of control. Whizzing by cars, it was probably doing upwards of eighty miles per hour. The bus began to veer from one lane to the other, like a giant python chasing down its prey.

Tucked away in the back of the bus, a few of my classmates hooped and hollered, enjoying what they figured was an exciting ride. I knew better though. Reflecting in the mirror above the driver, his golf ball sized eyeballs stared straight ahead. They suggested one thing: DOOM.

The driver now motioned for my teacher, Mr. Giff, to join him. Mr. Giff's pupils became the size of saucers. He peered into the mirror while bending his attention toward the driver. After speaking with the driver in hushed tones, Mr. Giff abruptly turned around.

"Can I have your attention, please!" Mr. Giff shouted. "I need you to brace yourselves. We're gonna crash!"

by Molly G. age 14

The yellow torpedo kept increasing in speed. The hollering turned into screams of panic. I kept my eyes on that mirror. Something told me that it was the key to our fate.

Then it happened. The right front tire of the bus dipped onto the road's shoulder, tipping the bus slightly onto two wheels. The driver quickly spun the wheel to the left. He battled against the beast to keep it from rolling over.

I stared into the mirror above the driver, hoping to see what he was going to do next. Then I closed my eyes and started to pray. Instantly I felt a sense of confidence that everything would be all right. At that point, the most remarkable thing happened. With my eyes still shut, I saw my body floating away. I felt myself move through the driver's mirror. Now I was sitting in his place. The driver was no longer there.

Grabbing the wheel, I realized there was no time to react, because the bus was heading for a collision. Confined to our metal prison, we rushed closer and closer to a humongous boulder. I then felt a tremendous jolt. My body shook violently. The sound of a single voice echoed throughout my head.

"Hey Space Head, wake up!"

It took a few seconds before I finally realized what happened. My best friend, Kyle, was trying to wake me. I had fallen asleep on the bus.

"We're almost there." Kyle said as he peered out his window.

I shook the cobwebs from my head and murmured, "Boy, that was some dream."

Scanning the bus to make sure all was well, I peeked off to my right, and Kate Ellis glanced back.

"'Bout time ya woke up, Parker." Kate said, smiling at me across the aisle.

I gave her a quick nod then closed my eyes. I tried to

relive what happened in my dream.

"Hey Kyle?" I asked, after a few moments passed.

Impatiently, Kyle turned from the window.

"Boy, did I have a bizarre dream…it seemed so real."

"I don't doubt it, Park; you were squirming like a worm in your seat."

"Really?"

"Oh yeah. But I figured I'd let ya sleep," Kyle returned to the window. "This field trip's gonna be awesome!"

"So we're real close to the Caverns?" I strained to get a better look out Kyle's window. Off to the left I could see the muddy Meramec River.

"That must be it, right there." Kyle pointed to the water outside of the front windshield.

I turned my head and my eyes caught the driver's mirror; the same one from my dream. I stared into the mirror. The driver stared into it as well. Our eyes locked. *Oh no, here we go again!* I thought. My dream crept back to me. Then the bus came to an abrupt halt and I heard Mr. Giff's voice.

"All right everybody. This is Meramec Caverns." Mr. Giff glanced briefly at his watch. "We have about fifteen minutes before our tour begins."

I poked Kyle in the ribs with a mischievous smile.

"Let's show these people what a great 4th grade class we have," Mr. Giff beamed. "Remember, make me proud that I'm your teacher and not sorry I took the job!"

"Yes sir," a few voices responded. But not mine of course.

As I stood, I motioned to Kate and Abby to walk in front of me. Kyle gave me a shove in the back.

"Why'd ya let them go first before us?" Kyle cried out.

"What's the difference?" I smiled. "We're all going to the same place."

Abby whispered something in Kate's ear. Kate just giggled. I pretended not to notice.

"See what you've started." Kyle scolded me. "We gotta lose them when we get in the caverns."

"Yeah...we will."

I stared at the two of them as they ran off ahead of us. There was something odd about Kate and Abby. On one hand, they could be as annoying as a little sister but on the other hand, they were actually kinda cool. And Kate, well, she was all right looking. For a girl. She didn't dress like the other girls. She was also tomboyish, with her long blonde hair usually in a ponytail. Yeah, she sometimes seemed like one of the guys.

Abby, though, was undeniably a girl. She likes pink. Yuck! And she never pulled her hair back like Kate. It was always long, straight, and black. And no matter what Abby did, her hair always got into whatever she was doing. Like into her food when she was eating. I remember the time she got paint on her hair because it dipped into the paint can. Boy that was a riot.

"Hey Finnegan!" I heard someone call out to me. I turned around, and it was Jason Jeffers. "Ya ever been to this place?"

I thought for second, and then answered. "Naw, but my dad has. He said it's pretty cool."

"Well, I heard it's HUGE," Jason shouted. "I also heard a couple of kids got lost one time when they got separated from their group."

"Lemme guess…and they were never found, right?" Kyle said mockingly.

I smiled at Kyle and was about to add something, but Jason ran up ahead.

"Ah, ya scared him off, Kyle."

"Some kids got lost, yeah right," Kyle countered. "What's he think we are? Couple of sissies?"

When Kyle and I got to the end of the line, it hit a snag

and we had to wait. My mind started to drift again as I stared at the back of Kyle's head. It kinda reminded me of a rock. It was shaped like a potato with a few bumps on it, and since he had a crew cut I could see the lumps stand out. That got me to thinking more about Kyle and what a good friend he was, even though he was kinda funny looking. Kyle liked to complain a lot, but there was not a better friend a guy could have. He always kept me laughing with his goofy personality. It somehow seemed to fit the shape of that head.

"Hey," Kyle turned around to face me. "What time's lunch anyway?"

"We just got here…we'll probably eat after the tour." I shook my head as the line started to move more quickly. When we reached the lobby, I saw Mr. Giff waiting for us.

"When we get inside," Mr. Giff announced, "I want everyone to follow me through the store lobby and into the beginning of the cavern." Glancing at Kyle and me, the Giff added. "This will be a field trip to remember!"

"So, do ya think it's gonna be a little spooky inside?" Kate nudged me.

As always, Abby stood right at her side. I sometimes wondered if they were separated Siamese twins.

"Of course," I replied. "It's a dark cave with bats and

spiders...

"And don't forget those lost kids," Kyle interrupted.

"Yeah they've got to be pretty angry and hungry after all this time," I added laughing.

"Well, if that's the case," Abby responded, "maybe we'll stick close to you guys."

"Hey, we're not gonna protect ya," Kyle jumped in.

Smirking, Kate countered. "Who says we'll be the ones who're afraid?"

Abby quickly grabbed Kate's arm and led her away, much too fast for either Kyle or me to answer.

"We'll see about that," Kyle snickered.

At about that time, Mr. Giff walked to the front of our group with someone who appeared to be our guide. Mr. Giff calmly motioned with his arms for everyone to calm down.

There was something about Mr. Giff that I liked. He rarely got angry, and he seemed to want to have fun. But I sensed he knew something we didn't. *I guess we were gonna find out soon enough,* I thought.

So It Begins

2

Standing before us, decked out in ranger green, was our tour guide. He reminded me of a drill sergeant looking over new recruits. His head was cocked to one side. He squinted with one eye, and the other seemed to bulge outward. To top it off, his mouth curled up toward the half shut eye. Scanning our faces, he certainly took his time to look us over. He kinda gave us all the creeps.

I turned to Kyle after he passed by us. Kyle quickly turned to look at me.

"Weird," I whispered.

"Yeah, something tells me this guy's been hanging out in the cavern a little too long."

"All right, let me have your attention!" our guide bellowed.

Boy did he have a powerful voice. He certainly got our attention.

"I'm Flynn, your guide for today."

"Flynn?" Kyle and I snickered. Mr. Giff must have heard us. He shot us a glimpse but quickly added a smile. Shrugging my shoulders, I stuck my hands in my pockets.

"I want to welcome all you fourth graders to Meramec Caverns," Flynn continued. "Today, we'll be going through one of Missouri's largest caves."

Kyle poked me. I figured he was thinking about the lost kids.

"As we proceed, I'll be turning lights on and off along the pathway. So, I'll need all of you to stick close, and pay attention." Flynn paused for a second to let that last statement sink in. "Needless to say I don't want any of you getting lost. But if you do…grab the handrails and feel your way back. Or you can scream, and we'll find you."

Kyle jabbed me again, and I knew he was gonna say something. "Is that what happened to those lost kids who were never found?" Kyle blurted out.

Turning abruptly, Flynn stared with his beady eye. Somehow he zeroed in on Kyle. "I can assure you," Flynn snapped. "We've never lost anyone here."

"At least not yet," Jason Jeffers added.

"All right, simmer down," Mr. Giff said. "We've got a lot to see and a lot to do."

Raising his arm and turning toward the cave, Flynn moved forward. Finally, the tour was starting. Flynn filled us in on various facts about the cavern as we walked along the lighted trail. We learned all about Jesse James and his famous escape to the cavern. Before long, we knew the history of the cavern's existence. It wasn't until we reached the area of the cave where the jagged rocks hung down from the ceiling that it started to get interesting.

Flynn called these rock formations, stalactites. I had no idea it took hundreds of years for them to develop. They kinda looked like brown icicles to me. That's also when we found out about the creatures that lived in the cavern. Kyle asked about them, and Flynn didn't hesitate to fill us in.

"Some of the creatures we've found living in the cavern range from bats, fish, spiders…"

Tapping Abby on the shoulder, I whispered. "Ohh, spiders." She didn't seem to appreciate it much.

Flynn continued, "And one of the most unusual creatures is the blind fish."

"Are you serious?" Jason blurted.

"Absolutely. Because of the darkness this fish has no eyes."

"How do they eat?" Abby asked.

"They eat whatever they can find."

"Better watch out, Abby," Kyle joked. "Ya might be on their menu!"

I looked over at Mr. Giff. He chuckled slightly. Scanning the water that was always flowing around us, I tried to see one of the eyeless fish. According to Flynn they were further down the cave, which was not part of the tour. Nonetheless, as we backtracked out of the stalactite room I continued to examine the water.

Nudging me, Kyle asked. "What're we looking for, Park?"

I hadn't realized it, but we were now at the back of the group.

"I'm trying to see one of those weird fish."

"Well, if we don't catch up we're gonna be in the dark. Flynn keeps turning the lights off behind us."

"No problem." I turned and smiled at Kyle. Then I snatched something out of my pocket.

"Hey, that a little flashlight?"

"You betcha. Something told me I should bring it along."

By this time we had stopped walking, and the crowd was much further up ahead. Then, all of a sudden, the lights went out! A fading glimmer of light in the distance was all we could see.

"Now we've done it!" Kyle blurted out. "We better get moving."

We heard a sound. A noise, we were both convinced, neither of us made.

"Psst, psst," came the sound.

"Did ya do that?" I asked Kyle nervously.

"Uh, nooo."

Then we heard it again, only this time we heard a voice too.

"Psst, Parker. Down here."

"Quick, Parker, shine your flashlight down by the stream."

Shaking, my fingers fumbled with the switch. Finally, I aimed it in the water. We didn't see it at first, but then the voice spoke up again.

"Over here, I'm over here, Parker."

Low and behold we saw it. It was one of those blindfish. Well, at least that's what we thought. It clearly didn't have any eyes.

"Ah, you found me," spoke the fish. "Don't mean to alarm you, Parker, but I need your help."

"Whoa, what's going on here?" Kyle spoke up. "Did ya

put that thing in the water?"

"I've been called many names before," the fish replied, "but never, *That Thing!*"

"I can't believe this!" I yelled in excitement.

"Yeah me neither," Kyle added nervously.

I turned to face Kyle while the glow of my flashlight illuminated our two faces.

"No, ya don't understand, Kyle. I think I know who this is."

"Now it's a who?" Kyle blurted.

I spun around aiming the light back on the fish, but I didn't need to. He was glowing in the darkness and lit the cavern around us. "Your name's Zeke, isn't it?"

"Zeke?!" shouted a confused Kyle.

I flashed the light between Kyle and me.

"Actually it is, son," came the fish's reply.

"This's too weird…you two actually know each other?"

"Well, not exactly," Zeke answered. "But I know his father."

I promptly turned the flashlight on Kyle.

"Kyle, I know this is strange and all, but Zeke's a creature from one of God's hidden worlds."

"The Clan of the Tree Travelers, to be precise," added Zeke.

"The what?" shouted Kyle.

"Trust me," I interrupted. "According to the story my dad told, Zeke took him and my Aunt Elizabeth on an awesome adventure when my dad was about our age."

"What for?" Kyle asked.

"So my dad could make a difference in the world. Does that sound right, Zeke?"

I could tell Kyle was having a hard time believing this, but then again we were talking to a fish. I began to wonder what Zeke needed from me, or from us for that matter. Right on cue, as if Zeke could read my thoughts, something bizarre happened. Zeke disappeared. Kyle and I were left standing by ourselves.

"Where'd he go?" Kyle asked.

Before I could comment, we heard Zeke's voice again. Only this time it came from above us.

"Up here boys!" Zeke called out.

Shining the light up at the ceiling, I saw nothing but rocks. Obviously Zeke was no longer gleaming.

"No, over here," came the voice again.

This time I moved the beam a little to my left. There he was, only now he was a bat. Jumping a few feet, Kyle was a little startled by Zeke's new appearance.

"How'd he do that?" Kyle called out.

"Lemme tell ya, it's probably not the last time he changes."

"Well, I'm not scared," Kyle said defiantly.

I grinned, and, I could've swore Zeke smiled back at me.

"So, what do ya need from us?" I asked. "Is there some kind of mission we need to go on?"

"Exactly...but first let me shed some more light." Kyle and I looked at each other and then back up at Zeke. He was dangling upside down from the ceiling and shimmering bright as ever.

"Parker, do you remember the dream you had this morning while riding on the bus?" Zeke asked.

"Sure I do, it was pretty weird...but how'd you know I had that dream?"

"That's not important, but there are two things about that dream that are keys to your quest."

"What two things?" I asked.

"The mirror above the drivers head, and the giant rock the bus was about to crash into."

I still wasn't sure what he meant by the mirror and the rock. Sure, they were part of my dream, but so what?

"You didn't tell me, ya had a dream about our bus

crashing," Kyle blurted out.

"I guess I didn't think it was that big a deal."

"It was," Zeke interrupted. "Unfortunately, that's all I can tell you at this time."

"Wait, what do ya mean?" I was getting confused.

"Yeah, don't leave us hanging," Kyle added.

"Remember these three things," Zeke paused before continuing. "There is something about the mirror that will give you your first clue."

"What else?" Kyle blurted.

"Quiet!" I replied, elbowing him.

"I can't help it, I'm excited."

"The second clue is to remember how I first appeared to you."

"Well, that's easy," Kyle shouted. "As a fish."

I aimed the flashlight straight into Kyle's eyes and he sheepishly turned his head downward. "Go on Zeke, what else?"

"Third, and most important…don't tell anyone else about this." And then he was gone. I shined the light all over the ceiling and then into the water, but Zeke was nowhere to be found.

"What're we gonna do?" Kyle asked excitedly, as he

grabbed me by my arm.

"We're gonna pay attention to the clues."

"And then what?"

I paused for a second, thinking about Kyle's question. Then I remembered Dad saying that God has a purpose for everything. I instantly knew what to say. "We take a leap of faith!"

It was at that point we heard a sound coming our way. Turning the flashlight off, I nudged Kyle forward.

"Wha, wha, where we going?" he stammered. "What if there are more talking creatures?"

"Don't worry about it. Something tells it's Mr. Giff or Flynn looking for us."

"Kyle? Parker? Are you two down here?" An intense beam of light found where we were standing.

Neither of us said a word.

The Riddle's Answer

3

It didn't take long for Mr. Giff to find us. The beam from his borrowed flashlight was the first thing we saw. But the oddest thing was that he didn't seem overly concerned about us being separated from the rest of the class. It was almost as if he expected it.

"You two better hustle up…the tour is taking off without you."

Following Mr. Giff, we arrived at the lighted portion of the cave. I have to admit being out of the dark was good. Glancing at Mr. Giff, Kyle and I watched him stare at the water. He appeared to be searching for someone or something. A moment passed, and he walked away.

"That's it?" Kyle whispered. "Mr. Giff's not gonna yell at us?"

"Beats me...I'm wondering what he was looking at."

Quietly we followed the rest of the tour, while still hanging toward the back. Flynn took us along a stream that seemed to lead to a bigger body of water. Only this water was still, kinda like a lake. Then we all stopped.

Whispering, Kyle asked. "So Park, what do ya think that the creature was talking about back there…you know, look for a mirror?"

"His name is Zeke," I replied. "As for a mirror, buddy, your guess is as good as mine."

"But he also said something about what he first looked like…"

"Yeah, he must have meant when he showed up as a fish."

Before we got a chance to continue our conversation Kate and Abby joined us.

"Where've you two been?" Kate asked.

"Ya guys get lost?" Abby added smiling.

"Ahh, nowhere," I blurted.

"Yeah, we were kinda hanging in the back," Kyle continued.

Kate's smirk suggested she didn't believe us. For some reason, she could always tell when I was up to something. I swear that girl knew me better than most of my friends.

"I guess we better keep our eyes on you two," Kate smiled. "You're up to something…I can tell."

"Look, don't bug us, okay!" Kyle bellowed.

Turning to whisper in Kyle's ear, I noticed Kate whisper something into Abby's.

"Whatever it is we're looking for, we better be sneaky," I said softly.

Kyle shot a glance over at the girls. They both started laughing. "All right then. Mirror, fish, fish, mirror." Kyle spoke to himself, but loud enough so I could hear him.

I scanned the entire cavern and noticed that nothing stood out. We were interrupted by our tour guide.

"This next stop is pretty interesting," Flynn announced. Everyone quickly focused attention on him. "When you look at this body of water, what do you notice?"

Someone shouted out, "It's not moving."

Another classmate announced, "It looks deep!"

I took another look at the water to see if I agreed. I thought about the two things Zeke said to look for.

"You're both right," Flynn answered. "But there are three things about this water that are of interest."

As soon as I heard Flynn say there are three things, my mind started to race.

Pointing towards the river, Flynn hesitated before continuing. "The first thing is that the water is not moving.

by Molly G. age 14

"Man, that's cold," Kyle blurted.

"The third and most unusual thing about this water is that it's an optical illusion."

Then it hit me! The water was the mirror!

"This water is called Mirror River," Flynn announced. "And it's an optical illusion because it's only sixteen inches deep."

Grabbing my arm and spinning me toward him, Kyle

obviously figured it out too. "That's it!" he whispered. "This is the mirror."

"And Zeke is somewhere in the river, as a fish," I added.

"Right you are," announced Zeke.

Quickly we turned our attention to the edge of the river. We could barely see him, but we knew it was Zeke.

"I thought you wanted this kept secret?" I whispered.

"Don't worry, you two are the only ones who can see and hear me," Zeke answered.

Looking at the others, I made sure no one was watching. The closest people to us were Kate and Abby. They seemed more interested in what Flynn was saying. "All right, now that we solved the riddle, what do ya need us to do?" I asked.

I glanced at Kyle, and he seemed eager to get involved.

"Jump in!" Zeke replied. "I have a quest for you."

"WHAT!" Kyle shouted.

I glanced over at the others and saw Kate staring back at me. "Ya knucklehead," I whispered to Kyle. "Ya wanna bring them over here?"

"Sorry…but he's crazy if he thinks we're gonna jump into that freezing water. Besides, you heard Flynn; it's only sixteen inches deep."

"Actually, it's much, much deeper," Zeke responded. "The cavern employees *think* it's only sixteen inches deep, but it's more."

"Well, even if it is, we'd freeze to death, Zeke," I whispered.

"OH, you two of such little faith. We live by faith, not by sight."

Scrunching his face, Kyle asked, "What's with the scripture?"

I paused for a second thinking about my own dad's experience and how valuable Zeke's scripture was to him when he went on his quest. Realizing no matter what we do it will truly be for a reason. I figured it would also just be a blast. "I'm in," I announced. "Where should I get in the water?"

"Ya gonna do this, Park? I mean, we have no idea what to expect."

Slapping Kyle on the back, I took a step toward the railing. "That's the adventure of it."

"Well, if you're going…I'm going too."

"Step over the railing and I'll take care of the rest," Zeke announced.

As soon as I was on the edge of the lake I waited for Kyle

to join me. Then something remarkable happened. All of a sudden we shrunk down to the size of a pebble. You should have seen the look on Kyle's face. Boy was he amazed.

Crouching down on my knees, I felt the water. It was freezing cold. What a rush! I couldn't wait to jump in; I stood poised on the water's edge.

Kyle was standing behind me when I heard him yell, "Whatta you two doing?" Before I could turn around I fell forward, plummeting toward the bottom of the lake. I looked up and saw not one body floating above me, but three. My fear turned to shock wondering what exactly happened. And for that matter, who pushed me in.

Zeke swam next to me and with his mouth he gestured to let the water in. To my relief, I quickly realized I could breathe under water. The other neat thing was that the water didn't feel cold at all.

What an experience, swimming and breathing under water; we were only the size of marbles! Catching up to the other three bodies in the water with me, I saw that they looked shocked. I showed them that they could breathe on their own by opening and closing my own mouth. Good thing I did, because Kyle was a dark shade of blue and about to burst from holding his breath.

Even though we could breathe, I was hesitant to try and talk. But I sure had a lot of questions to ask. Following after Zeke, we swam deeper and deeper. Soon we came across a dark cavern and stopped. Once again, Zeke motioned for us to follow as we entered total darkness. No one knew what to do or where to go next because we couldn't see.

Out of nowhere a light appeared a short distance away. Where it was coming from was anyone's guess. I figured it was Zeke, or at least I hoped it was. When I swam closer to the light I finally saw the others. We were drawn to the glow like four confused moths.

Sure enough, the source of light was coming from Zeke. Not only was he still a fish, but he had a long horn coming from the top of his head with a small round light on the end of it. I had to admit it was kinda ugly looking, a lot like the pictures I'd seen of deep-sea fish.

It didn't stop us from following him. He again motioned for us to do so. Before long we could see the end of the cavern entrance and brightness all about. Bobbing up and down in the water, we watched Zeke leap onto a bank of dry land.

Believe me; it didn't take much motivation to do the same. Finally out of the water, we stood dripping on a riverbank. Zeke was nowhere in sight.

Without really thinking, the four of us formed a giant group hug, happy to be out of the darkness and onto dry land. Then it hit Kyle and me. We quickly came to our senses and realized that two of our group shouldn't even be there.

"You're the ones who pushed us into the water!" Kyle shouted while pointing his finger at Kate and Abby.

"What do ya think ya were doing?" I added.

There we were, two boys standing across from two girls. We were angry, frightened and soaking wet. But before the girls had a chance to respond, we heard a loud swooshing noise from overhead. Glancing up we saw a giant bat swooping downward toward us.

Kate and I dropped quickly to the ground. Kyle and Abby jumped back into the water. I glanced over at Kate. We now crawled toward each other. I could hear Kyle shouting for us to join them as he and Abby treaded water, side by side.

The bat landed. It was within a few feet of Kate and me. Then I realized who it was. Getting back up on my feet, I looked down at Kate. "It's all right, it's only Zeke."

"Who's Zeke?" Kate asked nervously.

"I am," Zeke announced. "Hey you two, you can come out of the water. It's all right."

Zeke motioned with one of his wings for Kyle and Abby to join us.

"Can someone tell me what's going on?" Kate asked, brushing mud from her clothes.

"All I know is that we're on some sort of quest with Zeke here." Kyle and Abby had joined us at this point. "Since you two insisted on following us…I guess now you're part of the team."

Glancing over at Kyle, I could tell he was still a little put out with Abby.

"Right you are!" Zeke announced. "Allow me to introduce myself to you young ladies." Abby and Kate stared at Zeke in amazement. "My name is Ezekiel, only you may call me Zeke, for short. I am from the clan of the Tree Travelers…"

"The what?" Abby blurted.

"The Tree Travelers," Zeke continued. "We are a civilization from one of God's hidden worlds."

"What do ya mean hidden world?" Kate asked.

"Well, amazingly to you all I'm sure; there are numerous hidden civilizations that few humans know about…"

"So you're saying there are others who know about these, these hidden worlds?" Kate interrupted.

"There are a few." Winking at me, Zeke added. "Right, Parker?"

Needless to say, all three of my friends turned to look at me, as if I had all the answers. All I could do was smile back at them.

"You see kids; a long time ago Parker's dad went on a quest with me to help solve a problem in four different hidden civilizations. Now it's time for you four to help solve a problem in one hidden world."

"But why do you need all four of us?"

Pointing at the girls, Kyle asked. "And why them?"

"All I can say is that each of you will play a crucial role in this adventure…and all of you will help solve the problem," Zeke answered.

"What problem?" Abby whined.

"And how do we solve it?" Kyle chimed.

"Let us begin our quest so we may find out. First, I want you four to climb onto my back. You will need to hold on tight…for where we're going will be nothing like where you came from. Now, here's a riddle for you to ponder…

Although it may seem we shall soar up, high,
It is straight ahead we must go.

For we are about to enter a hidden world,

That only you shall know.

⤞⤝

Turning to face me, Kate asked. "Does he always talk in riddles?"

"I don't know," I shrugged. "I just met Zeke a little while ago."

Zeke extended his wing down toward the ground and waited till we were all on his back. We clung to him for dear life as we sat in one straight row. Who knew where he was taking us next.

by Kate G. age 10

The First Obstacle

Our journey with Zeke was actually an extraordinary one. No sooner did he take off flying upward than he quickly swooped down heading straight for a wall of rocks. Almost as if in unison we all screamed at the top of our lungs for fear of crashing into the wall.

Kate, who was sitting behind me, loosened her grip on Zeke's skin and grabbed both of my arms. It didn't help that she screamed directly into my right ear. I was as frightened as she. Then the most remarkable thing happened. The wall got closer and closer to us, and a small crevice appeared. It couldn't have been any wider than a couple of inches. But it was wide enough for a bat to fly through. A bat flying sideways with kids the size of marbles on his back, that is.

Good thing I had a firm grasp of Zeke because we were all flying catawampus. But the best part was what appeared on the other side. Zeke gracefully landed and extended his wing for us to climb down. We realized we were in another cavern. Only this cavern seemed endless, and was different from the one we came from. Much different.

We were entirely surrounded by walls of rock in every color of the rainbow. The entrance led us into a massive valley. To the left stood a mountain that glistened in hues of red and orange. To the right of us were meandering hills with wisps of white surrounded by shades of blue. It was almost as if the sky were lying on its side. Directly in front of us was a beautiful shimmering lake that constantly changed colors from gold to emerald green and back again.

Rising up from the lake were hundreds of stalagmites that emitted a brilliant light. The stalagmites lit up everything around and allowed us to see this fascinating world. And above all else was a ceiling made totally of stalactites, reaching down towards the lake. Only these stalactites were not like the ones from the original cavern. You could see right through them. They appeared to be made of glass.

"Where are we?" Kate exclaimed in awe.

Our mouths were wide open in amazement.

"This is the majestic world of Crystal Lake," Zeke announced. "We now begin our journey to find the Ragamite and Dolamite creatures."

"The Rag a what?" Kyle replied.

"Don't worry," Zeke laughed. "You'll soon meet them."

"We will?" Looking about, Abby struggled to see. "How will we know who they are?"

"You'll know," Zeke answered. "But first we must set out for their villages. We must climb Onyx Mountain. Then, along the way you will be challenged with your first series of tests."

"Wait a minute Zeke; you didn't say anything about some tests." I clamored.

With arms crossed, Kyle added. "Yeah, I'm not ready for a bunch of tests!"

"You're right," countered Zeke. "I believe I said you must solve a problem."

Glancing at each other, Kyle and I figured that we straightened him out.

"But, the problem cannot be solved until you know the answer…"

This time we all looked at each other knowing that the next thing Zeke said might not be good.

"And the answer will be found from being tested."

"Let me get this straight…in order for us to help these creatures we need to figure out an answer, to some test?" I asked.

Moving in front of me, Kate added, "And in order to get the answer, we have to be tested somehow?"

"Precisely," Zeke replied.

"But what if we fail the tests?" Kyle whined.

"That is one reason I selected the four of you. Four strands of rope are stronger than one."

"Oh, I get it." I nodded my head in agreement. "Each of us has a different strength."

"And together we can come up with the answer to help the, what did you call them, Ragamites?" Kate asked.

"Now you understand. But we must go, for time is short, and our journey is long."

Placing his hand on my shoulder, Kyle said, "Parker, I'm worried about this…I mean, how will we know what to do?"

"Yeah, it's not as if we know what our strengths are," chimed Abby.

"I can't believe you two!" Kate threw her hands up in the air. "We have a chance to go on an awesome adventure, and help some civilization out." Glaring at Kyle and Abby, she continued. "God selected us for a reason and I, for one, am going to do my best."

I glanced over at Zeke as he patiently waited for our conversation to end. I could tell he liked what he heard from

Kate. At least two of us were raring to go.

"To get to Onyx Mountain we must first cross Crystal Lake," Zeke announced.

"Great, can you turn into a speed boat?" Kyle snickered.

"Sorry son, I have been given the power to become any *living* creature, only."

Jumping in, I suggested, "Well in that case how about becoming a dolphin and we'll hitch a ride from you."

"Or why don't we fly on your back again?" Abby added.

"That would be too easy," Zeke chortled. "I have something different in mind."

We all stared at Zeke, expecting him to transform into something spectacular, something that would blow us away. Then he changed. Not into something we had never seen before, but into something so familiar, that at first we were all a little disappointed. Zeke became a frog, only one that was much bigger than us, giving that we were all but the size of pebbles.

"You turned into a frog!" Kyle shouted. "What's so different about that?"

Opening his enormous mouth, Zeke replied. "Have you ever ridden on a frog before, young man?"

"Well, no I haven't, but I figured you'd at least become

something unusual."

"So are we supposed to climb on your back and hop over the lake?" Abby joked.

"Yes and no," Zeke answered.

Pointing to the other end of the lake, I said, "There's no way you can hop clear across this lake, is there?"

"Actually part of the quest requires us to utilize what we have in front of us. So, we will do some hopping, but we must hop from one stalagmite to another."

"Why can't we swim across?" Kate motioned with her arms.

"I was waiting for someone to ask that question…the reason is, if you go into the water, you will change color like the water."

"You mean if we fall in we'll became gold or green?" I asked.

"Exactly." Hopping from one spot to another, Zeke added. "So if the only way to get across Crystal Lake is to go from one stalagmite to the next. Then we must hop."

Well that certainly got our attention. Each of us approached the water's edge and watched as the lake continued to change from gold to green and back again. It was a pretty cool sight, but knowing that we could become one of those colors permanently was a little unnerving.

Turning around, I faced Zeke. We had no choice but to put our trust in him. "I really hope you're sure-footed." I turned back to look at the changing water again. "I'd hate to fall in and become green."

"Yeah, I don't think I'd wanna be gold either," Kyle added.

"Relax, you should be okay," Zeke laughed.

Shaking her head, Abby said, "I'm glad you think this is funny."

"Let's go for it!" Kate cried out.

Within seconds, we were all on Zeke's back. Fortunately he wasn't slimy, so we didn't slip off.

"Hang on any way you can, 'cause I will be jumping forward, sideways, up and down."

"Talk about a leap of faith," I joked.

"Good one Parker, but more like many leaps," Kate laughed.

Before we knew, we were off. The first stalagmite was pretty close to shore, so Zeke had no problem reaching it. The second was straight up and down, so we were momentarily caught sideways.

"OHHH, I think I'm slipping!" Kyle yelled.

"Hold on Kyle!" Zeke called out.

Soaring through the air, we headed for another stalagmite.

This one was a little better, although we were still leaning. By the time, we were half way across the lake I felt like a Mexican jumping bean. Fortunately, Zeke stopped to give us a breather.

"Almost there," Zeke announced. "Are you doing okay?"

Reaching for his stomach, Kyle mumbled, "I'm a little queasy."

"Hey!" Abby shouted. "If you think you're gonna get sick you better not blow this way."

Everyone chuckled, except for poor Kyle.

"Off we go!" Zeke yelled.

Zeke didn't give us any time to prepare for his sudden departure. Jumping sideways again didn't help either. Suddenly Kate lost her grip and started to fall off Zeke's back. Reaching out, she screamed for someone to grab it.

Amazingly, Kyle was the first one to reach her. The panic in Kate's eyes must have taken his mind off his own troubles. Unfortunately, the angle at which Kate was dangling forced Kyle to start to slip, as well.

Now we were in a real precarious situation. Kate lingered so close to the water that she was pulling Kyle along with her.

"Help me! Help me! Please don't let go, Kyle."

"I'm slipping guys!" Kyle shouted.

Grabbing Kyle's left arm, Abby shouted, "I gotcha!"

"Hurry Zeke!" I yelled. "They're all slipping."

There was no response from Zeke as he continued to hop from one stalagmite to the next. The only thing that looked promising was that we were real close to the shore. I had to think of something quick, but what? My friends were slipping toward the water, and I didn't know what to do. Then I thought about what Zeke said earlier. Four strands of rope are stronger than one. If I only had some rope.

Searching all about me, I came up with a solution. I could use my belt. As fast as possible, I removed my belt and extended it down toward Kate to grab. "Kate! Grab my belt, and I'll try to pull you up."

Bug eyed, Kate cried out. "Whatever you do, Kyle, don't let go of my hand."

"I gotcha Kate," Kyle replied confidently.

Skimming the water with her seat bottom, Kate grasped my belt buckle with her right hand.

"Hurry, please hurry! I can feel my pants touching the water."

I pulled with all my strength and within seconds Kate was back on top of Zeke's back. Only now she was facing me rather than facing forward. Immediately she let go of

Kyle's hand. Wasting no time, Abby pulled Kyle back up as well. Hopping to the safety of land, we were now all riding on top of Zeke. Of course, none of us wasted time bolting for the solid ground.

"We made it! We made it!" Abby shouted.

We all jumped up and down, dancing and laughing out loud. Then, as if realizing we were caught on camera doing something wrong, Kyle and I broke away from the group. We heard Zeke speak.

"Now that's what I call teamwork. You all did magnificently out there."

"You mean to tell me you knew what was going on?" Kate interrupted.

"Of course...I just couldn't intervene."

Jumping in front of Zeke, Kyle said, "So you're saying you couldn't help us?"

"As soon as the quest started it was up to you to solve all dilemmas that you encounter. I merely provide clues and transportation, if you will."

"It sounds like it's up to us from this point on," Abby whined.

"Basically, yes...but don't worry, you will not face anything that you cannot handle. Trust in the Lord with all your heart and lean not on your own understanding."

Smiling, Kate replied, "Proverbs 3:5, right?"

"Very good, young lady."

"Hey, it's easy to quote scripture," Kyle scolded. "But we're not the ones who can turn into almost anything we want."

I realized this conversation wasn't going well, so I decided to speak up. "Hey guys, think about it...we worked together, and everything turned out."

Gesturing toward the lake, Kate added. "Yeah, if we made it across that goofy lake, well, we can handle whatever comes next."

Abby and Kyle started laughing. They were actually pointing at Kate. Then I saw what they were laughing at.

"Uh, Kate. You know how your pants were white when we started this adventure."

"What are you getting at, Parker?" Kate asked confused.

Pointing at Kate's bottom, Kyle laughed. "Your backside is green!"

Kate tried her best to look behind her and she caught a glimpse of emerald green on her seat. "Wow, talk about a close call. I suppose it's permanent."

"Better the pants than you," I chuckled.

"Hate to break up the fun, but it's time to move on," Zeke interrupted. "We have a huge mountain to climb before we will arrive at the Ragamite Village."

Glancing off in the distance I asked, "Is that Onyx Mountain in front of us?"

"Indeed it is."

Standing in our path was a tremendous snow-white mountain that appeared to reach into the heavens.

"Can't you turn into a pack mule or something, so we can ride you up the mountain?" inquired Kyle.

"I could…but since you can all walk on your own, I can't help you."

"Isn't there another way?" Abby shook her head. "I mean do we have to climb this gigantic hill?"

"There are always OTHER ways," Zeke said, winking at us.

"Here he goes again being mysterious," Kyle replied.

"I kinda like it," Kate chimed.

"Yeah…it keeps us on our toes," I added.

Leaping toward the mountain, Zeke cried out, "Time to go!"

That obviously got our attention. We all focused on Zeke expecting him to turn into something else, or start hopping upward.

"First a riddle, and then we'll leave," Zeke announced.

If help is what you hope to find,

To tell you where to go.

Then seek the watchman on the wall,

To find what you need to know.

5

"What's that suppose to mean?" Kyle asked. "What watchman? What wall?"

Zeke stared at us without replying. I knew he wasn't going to give us any clues, other than what he said. I vaguely remembered that the watchmen were from the Old Testament, but finding them was another story.

"Hey guys…do you remember the stories of the watchman from our Bible lessons on the Old Testament? You know, in the books of the prophets."

"Yeah, like in Ezekiel where he was a spiritual watchman?" Kate answered.

Looking at Zeke, I could see he was pleased with our conversation. Then it hit me. I had a feeling I might be on to something. Approaching Zeke, I asked, "Isn't the name Zeke, short for Ezekiel?"

Zeke turned his head sideways and did something completely unexpected. Catching all of us off guard, he transformed himself into a new creature.

"Why did you turn yourself into a mouse?" Abby cried out.

Twitching his little whiskers, Zeke said, "Not a mouse, but a mole."

"Does this mean you're going to give us a clue how to get through the mountain?" Abby asked.

"It is only because Parker solved my riddle that I will indeed show you a short-cut through the mountain."

"I did?"

"Sure you did," Kate gestured. "You knew that his real name is Ezekiel, and the prophet Ezekiel from the Bible was considered a watchman. Right?"

"Right again! I think you children are starting to get the hang of this quest...so let us proceed straight through Onyx Mountain." We headed forward and Zeke looked over his shoulder. "On the other side is where your biggest challenge awaits," he added.

Since we were still tiny in size we had no difficulty following Zeke through a small crevice into the mountain. It was pitch dark, so we all held hands and walked sideways. Remembering my flashlight, I pulled it out and stayed in the back.

Even with the minimal light provided by the flashlight, there was an eerie feeling along the path. My mind started to play tricks on me. I could've swore I saw tiny pairs of florescent eyes staring back.

Fear quickly gave way to nervousness. The eyes disappeared, and I thought about what Zeke said about facing our biggest challenge yet. What kind of challenge would there be and who were these creatures we were suppose to help? Beckoning us, a light shined up ahead.

"Finally!" Kyle shouted. "The other side of the mountain."

As we dashed through the opening we discovered a totally different world than where we came from. The sky above us was now a deep blue with sparkles; Twinkling, tiny specks of stars, even though it was daylight. There was no sun but plenty of light. I wondered if this is what heaven is like.

The entire landscape before us was incredible. The ground was a mixture of clay and sand with a reddish brown hue. There was an infinite number of mountain peaks, as far as the eye could see. And each peak had an orange tinge, like glowing embers in a fire.

It was much warmer here than where we came from.

Dripping from my brow were tiny beads of sweat. I turned around to ask Zeke a question. That's when I suddenly became frightened.

"What happened?" I shouted.

The others turned in unison to see what I was shouting about.

"What, what are you talking about?" Abby asked.

"There," I pointed. "The opening...it's gone!"

Kyle and Kate ran to where we entered. Sure enough, the opening was no longer there; nothing but solid rock all around the spot.

"Zeke?" Kate asked alarmingly. "What happened to the entrance...you know, the opening into the mountain?"

Zeke's little whiskers bounced up and down as he prepared himself to speak. "That passage is now gone. You must find another way back when the time comes."

"Another way back?" Kyle moaned. "The only way back is over that blasted mountain."

"Calm down, Kyle," I jumped in. "We found the way here and we can surely find a way back."

Abby and Kyle continued to complain about our present situation while Kate and I tried to intervene. The booming sound of our voices seemed to carry. I suddenly realized why. In a blink of an eye we all returned to our normal sizes. We were now ordinary kids again.

We were abruptly distracted by something else. Something even more perplexing. Echoing from far away was the sound of a horn, or some kind of instrument. The sound would last for a few seconds and then stop. Then it started up again about ten seconds later.

Cupping his hand around his ear, Kyle shouted, "That sounds like some kind of signal."

"Sorta like a warning sound," Abby added.

"What kind of warning?" I asked. "And is it meant for us?"

We stared at Zeke for an answer, but he continued to twitch his little nose hairs. "Don't be alarmed by that sound," he finally announced. "We have been spotted, and now I know where we must head."

"Spotted!" shouted Abby. "I don't like the sound of that."

"Who spotted us?" Kyle asked.

"One of the watchmen on the towers." Zeke took a moment to listen before adding. "I only hope…"

"You hope what?" Kate asked in an excited voice.

"I hope it is a watchman from the Ragamite clan. For it is he whom we seek."

"Wha, what if it's not?" Kyle stammered.

"Then we have been found by the Dolamites…it is they we wish to avoid."

Standing before the others I addressed our protector. "Zeke, we're trusting you. What should we do next?"

"First of all, from this point on you must all speak softly."

Simultaneously Kate and I stared at Kyle and Abby. It was those two who needed to stop arguing.

"Next, you all need to follow closely behind me. We will try to sneak up on the watchman."

"Then what?" I whispered.

"When we get close enough I will know if he is Ragamite or Dolamite. If he is Ragamite, we will approach…"

Interrupting, Kate asked. "And if he isn't?"

Zeke paused before speaking; he seemed to be assessing the situation. "We will run!"

No one said a word. The real test was starting. Silently and tentatively we followed Zeke as he made his way from one boulder to the next. The sheer size of every rock cropping easily hid us. But open space made us too vulnerable.

The closer we got the clearer the horn sounded. No one

knew what to expect next, including Zeke. Movement above caught our attention. Then we saw him. Blending perfectly with the side of a hill was the watchman. His tower had to be at least one hundred feet high. Yet, it was his horn that stood out the most. Carved of wood, it measured at least four feet long. He raised the horn every few seconds to make the sound that blasted across a valley. It was then we scampered closer to the tower. Eventually we were right below the tower when the blasts stopped. Like frightened little mice, we froze in our tracks. We tried our best not to make any sounds. The watchman stopped.

"What's he doing?" Kate whispered, to no one in particular.

Whispering to Zeke, I asked, "Don't we need to get closer? You know, to see if he's the good guy?"

Without warning the tower shook violently. Thundering about us the ground stirred like an earthquake. Something, or someone had leaped out of the tower. Standing directly behind us now, we could hear it breathe.

Tiny hairs stood straight up on the nape of my neck. Slowly, we all turned to stare at a creature we could never have imagined existed. But there he was, towering over us, silent.

Without hesitating, Zeke transformed into a new creature, one that rivaled the watchman's height and size. Zeke became a Kodiak bear. He stood eye to eye with the watchman.

The watchman was staring straight at us. He was made of solid stone. His reddish brown color sorta looked like clay. He still had the appearance of a human, with arms and legs; only every single part of him was stone and rock. Blending in with his surroundings, much like a buck in the thick of a forest, the only thing that stood out was his fiery red eyes. Something about this watchman told us he was the one we were seeking. He and Zeke continued to stare at each other waiting for the other to speak.

Finally in a voice that sounded like deep echoes across a gravel pit, half words, half noise, the watchman spoke.

"You are the ones we have waited for? The ones who must speak to our leader?"

Assuring us with a wink, Zeke took a step back. He stood along side the four of us.

"I am Ezekiel, from the clan of the Tree Travelers. These four are humans who have been sent to help your clan."

The watchman towered over us. He hesitated before bending down to get a better look. His legs of stone flexed.

Now, he was close to our heights. The watchman's granite hands cupped something. He extended them in our direction. Then, he uncurled his stony fingers and an object appeared. It was a container of some sort. The watchman held it up. Attached to the top of the object were four strings. He held the container by the strings, and it dangled before our eyes. I could now see it was a bottle roughly eight inches long with a wide bottom and thin neck. The bottle was shiny and silver. I figured it must be made of some kind of metal.

As it dangled from the strings, the bottle swirled gently back and forth. It seemed to catch the rays of stars above. An array of colors appeared from the bottle each time it swayed. It was almost hypnotizing when you stared at it.

Finally, the watchman spoke again. "You are to take this container with you wherever you go."

Confused by his statement, we all glanced at each other.

Pointing with a stony finger, the watchman said, "When you reach the village of the Ragamites, it is then your true quest begins."

"What are we supposed to do with the bottle?" Abby interrupted.

Holding the container closer to us, once again it swayed from its strings. An assortment of colors washed over the surrounding area.

Ignoring Abby and directing his answer to Zeke, the watchman continued. "You must convince my clan to repent of their sin…"

"What sin?" Kyle blurted out.

For the first time, the watchman revealed a human expression. The fire in his eyes diminished, and they became sullen. Frowning, he hesitated before he spoke.

"My people…have fallen into the worshipping of an idol…they have turned away from God!"

"So we're here to convince them to abandon their sinful way and turn back to God?" Kate asked.

A glow returned to the watchmen's gaze.

"That is your goal," the watchman added, nodding his head. "But…you only have a limited amount of time."

"How much time?" I asked.

The watchman turned his attention from us and glanced up at the sky. He seemed to be meditating, and he said nothing for many seconds. Finally, glancing at the four of us, he motioned with his other hand toward the strings holding up the container.

"You will have until the four strings are cut from the container…if you do not succeed before the last string disappears, then your time will be up."

"And then what?" Kyle shouted.

Sighing, the watchman's head drooped. "The Dolamite clan will attack my people, and the Ragamites will be no more!"

My jaw felt as if it dropped to the bottom of a pit. I looked over at Kate, and her eyes were as big as dinner plates. We turned toward Zeke looking for confirmation. The watchman spoke one more time, and added, "But, if you four are successful…".

Now he had us eagerly waiting.

"A seal to this container will open. Inside you will find the answer to your way back home."

Of course, the obvious question everyone wanted to ask was, *will we still get home if we fail?* Almost as if the watchman were reading our minds, he continued. "If your quest fails, you will of course still be able to return to your home…but you must then find the way back on your own."

Sitting down, and shaking his head back and forth, Kyle blurted, "Whoa! This is too much for me."

Abby and Kate quickly joined him.

"So let me get this straight," I said, looking back and forth between Zeke and the watchman. "Somehow we need to convince the Ragamites to quit worshipping someone or something other than God. But we have to do it before the four strings disappear, right?" Placing my hands on my hips, I continued, "If we do, we find some message in that bottle and it will tell us how to get back to our classmates?"

"Exactly," replied Zeke.

"But if we don't convince them," Kate stood to her feet, "they get attacked by some other creatures and get destroyed?"

"That is true," the watchman answered.

"So, why would God want us? I mean, we're kids," I said, to no one in particular.

Jumping up, Kyle asked, "Yeah, why us?"

"You will soon find out," the watchman responded.

"Oh great, let me guess, you're gonna give us some riddle," Abby interjected.

Turning away from us, the watchman pointed off in the distance. All five of us approached him and stood alongside. The watchman spoke a final time. "You must head that way to reach my village of Dedan. There you will find our leader King Teman. Then it will be up to you." The watchman paused, keeping us hanging on his next words. "If, you arrive quickly you will not lose a string…but if you are delayed."

The watchman then crouched as low as he could go to the ground. Then instantly, he sprung upward towards the top of the tower. His sudden disappearance startled us all. One moment he was standing next to us, and the next he was gone.

"Wait!" Abby cried out. "How could we be delayed?"

But the watchman was nowhere to be seen. Kate and I turned our attention to Zeke. It was up to him to guide us the rest of the way.

The Dolamites

6

"Zeke?" I asked, "what exactly did the watchman mean by being delayed?"

"There is the possibility that the Dolamites, the clan that the watchman spoke of, may know of our presence."

I turned to see the reaction of my friends and was met by blank stares. I returned my focus to Zeke.

"If they find us, they may delay us," Zeke continued.

"How? How would they delay us?" Abby asked.

Zeke paused for a moment before continuing. It was obvious he didn't feel comfortable delivering this next bit of information. "They would delay us, by capturing us."

"What?" Kyle screamed.

"Shh, quiet Kyle!" Holding her finger up to her lips, Kate added, "We don't want to give ourselves away."

"It is the Dolamites' goal to rule over the Ragamites," Zeke explained. "If they find us they will likely assume we are here to prevent that…thus capturing us would be to their advantage."

"If that's the case," I said, "we better do our best to not be found."

"That's right," Kate interrupted. "We can't afford to lose any strings before we have a chance to speak to the Ragamites."

"So that's it huh?" Kyle shook his head. "We take our chances sneaking into the Ragamite Village and hope that along the way the bad guys don't find us? We need a better plan."

Standing defiantly Kate exclaimed, "No! We not only need a plan...we need to pray."

"Excellent idea," Zeke responded. "Who would like to start?"

We all looked around at each other, seeing if someone wanted to begin. It didn't take long before Kate spoke up. "I'll start."

"And...I'll finish," I added.

Kate smiled at me. I sheepishly returned the gesture.

"Dear Lord," she started, "we don't know why you picked us to be here, or what you wish us to do. But we put our faith in your hands...and trust that you will guide us to safety, and somehow help the Ragamites repent from their sin."

There was a slight pause from Kate's prayer, so I took the opportunity to jump in.

"And Father, all we ask is that ya show us a sign, or something. I guess what I'm trying to say is, if ya want us to help these people…show us the way and we'll do everything we can. Oh, and keep us safe and please return us home soon. Amen."

"You can't ask for more than that," Zeke responded, turning himself into yet another creature. This time he became a cat, very furry, yet sleek. He was black, brown, and gray all blended together. He also had the signature marking of a Mancoon. A distinctive "M" was stamped across his feline forehead.

"What? Now you're a cat!" Abby shouted.

"We will need all the keen senses of a feline to detect the Dolamites," Zeke spoke up. "Since they too are made of rock, the sense of smell is of no use. But my sense of hearing and sight are dramatically enhanced as a cat."

"Good thinking Zeke," Kyle chimed in. "I remember learning in science class that a cat has the keenest sense of hearing. Maybe he will be able to hear them first."

Grabbing the attention of everyone present Kate said, "Well, that means the rest of us have to be as quiet as possible."

"Follow me," Zeke spoke up.

I decided that I would hold onto our mysterious bottle and we headed out in the direction the watchman pointed towards. As we walked onward, I quickly tucked it away into my pants pocket. We weren't sure what to expect, but at least our prayers made us feel better. We walked for a long time, following closely behind Zeke. No one spoke a word. We all tried to be as silent as possible.

But something didn't seem right. It felt like eyes were watching us every step of the way. Although we didn't see anything unusual, it was a little unnerving that Zeke constantly stopped and scanned the rocks surrounding us. It was almost as if he, too, sensed something was not right.

We eventually came to a point where we had to pass through a narrow passage that led between two tall walls of rock. Single file, we all marched on. Zeke was in the lead followed by Kate, myself, Abby and finally Kyle in the rear.

Then it happened! Without making a sound, both Abby and Kyle vanished. Coming to life, two Dolamite soldiers emerged from the walls. They snatched Kyle and Abby and carried them away. By the time we came to the end of the passageway, it was too late.

"Oh, no!" Kate frantically turned about. "Where's Abby

and Kyle?"

"They were right behind me," I answered, but I saw nothing.

"We need to go back!" Kate shouted. "We need to find them."

Pouncing in front of us, Zeke blocked our paths. "You cannot," he announced. "Although your first reaction is to look for them, I can assure you, you will not find Kyle and Abby."

"What'ya mean? Are you trying to tell us they're gone... that's it, time to move on?" I demanded.

"The Dolamites will not harm them. God will protect them."

Placing her hands on her hips, Kate sneered. "How can you be sure? I thought *you* were supposed to protect us!"

Zeke waited for us to calm down. When he felt we were ready to listen, he spoke again. "I know this may be hard to understand, but this is all part of the plan. Kyle and Abby are safe. It is necessary for them to be in the hands of the Dolamites at this time."

"But why?" Kate cried out. "You're right, I don't understand."

Tilting his head slightly, Zeke paused before saying,

"All Christians must trust that God is directing all things according to his purposes. And you two must now put your complete trust in Him. No matter what happens next."

Then something occurred to me. Reaching into my pocket, I fumbled around with the bottle before finally pulling it out. I then held it up in front of us.

"Oh no," Kate spoke first.

"The bottle...we lost a string," I announced.

Throwing her hands up in the air, Kate moaned. "But it's not our fault."

"Maybe not, but we were delayed...and we were warned."

"Now we must pick up the pace," Zeke proclaimed. "Time is not on our side."

"And neither are the Dolamites," I added.

***

Kyle and Abby were led away blindfolded. Even though they were not able to see, they could tell they were obviously moving. They rode on some strange kind of cart. It seemed different because there was no bouncing up and down like one would experience if riding in a vehicle or wagon. Instead, the vehicle glided, as if on air.

"Kyle! Kyle, are ya there?" cried Abby.

"I'm here. Are you all right?"

"Yeah, I think so…but what about the others?"

"I don't think they're here."

It didn't take long before Kyle and Abby could hear the sounds of many voices. It sounded like lots of people moving about. A distinctive voice cried out as soon as their vehicle stopped. "Take them to the king."

A guard removed their blindfolds. Standing before them was a massive creature. It was much larger than the watchman they encountered earlier, but built along the same lines—made of solid rock with a blackish gray coloring. In a gravelly voice, it spoke. "Come with me and you will not be harmed." The creature motioned for Kyle and Abby to follow.

"Where are we?" Abby asked.

"Your guess is as good as mine." Wide eyed, Kyle paused. "But something tells me we've been captured by the Dolamites."

Feeling a sense of peace fall upon her, Abby looked Kyle squarely in the eyes. "I don't know about you…but for some strange reason, I'm not scared."

"Yeah, I know what you mean, in some weird way.

But when I look around us, this place almost seems like bizarre'o'land."

Snickering, Abby glanced around at the strange village before her. Many of the rock-like creatures were walking about and none of them seemed to pay any attention to Kyle and Abby. About the only thing they had in common though, was that Kyle and Abby could understand what the Dolamites were saying.

When they were led into a huge building and up a series of steps, Kyle and Abby were instructed to stop. The Dolomite opened two massive doors. The room inside was cavernous. Moving forward, Kyle and Abby craned their necks at the room's sheer size.

"King Cyrus will address you momentarily," the guard announced.

"King Cyrus?" Kyle scoffed. "Where have I heard that name before?"

"Shhhh, he might hear you."

"So what," Kyle shook his head. "This whole place seems too weird to me."

"Kyle! If you get us in trouble…"

Their conversation was interrupted by the announcement of King Cyrus' arrival. Her mouth hung wide open and Abby avoided looking at Kyle for fear of laughing out loud.

Making his entrance into the great room, King Cyrus was a sight to behold. He was much smaller than the guards surrounding him. In fact, he couldn't be seen until the guards moved away from him.

Along with his short stature, King Cyrus wore the oddest-looking crown on his head. It actually looked like a bowl with a bunch of colorful feathers shooting out from it. Draped around his shoulders was a cape made of leaves. The leaves were green and clashed with the king's colorful crown.

The king had what appeared to be a scepter in his stony hand. Only this scepter was not made of crystal or jewels like one would think. It was a long piece of rotting driftwood that stood taller than him.

Kyle and Abby did their best to keep from laughing out loud. Even though the king appeared goofy, they still needed to show him respect.

"Bow down to King Cyrus!" a guard announced.

The king held his head up in a lofty way, and Abby and Kyle wondered if they should bow. The king's guard bent down and whispered to them, "You must bow in his presence."

"Oh, sorry," Kyle replied.

They both got down on their knees. Then the king spoke.

"You may rise," he announced, but not in a gravelly voice like the others. The sound was a high pitch, almost like a child who inhaled some helium.

That put Kyle over the edge. He burst out into laughter. Abby tried her best to control herself. Judging by the king's face, she could tell he wasn't amused.

Rising to her feet, Abby cried out, "Oh great King Cyrus, please excuse my friend. He is a well noted jester in the land from where we came from."

Kyle looked up at Abby with a quizzical expression.

Whispering to Kyle Abby said, "Follow along, all right?"

"We only wish to please you and make ya laugh out loud with us," Abby continued.

By this time, Kyle had composed himself. He then stood alongside Abby.

"Now what?" Kyle hushed.

"You may approach me," the king announced.

Giggling once again, Kyle did his best to keep a straight face. Between his appearance and his high-pitched voice, it was hard to do. Drawing nearer to the king, Kyle and Abby saw the enormous contrast between him and his guards. The king's outfit was so flamboyant, and his physical size was twice as small as any other Dolamite. It certainly made Kyle and Abby wonder how he ever became king.

Motioning with his scepter, the king asked, "So you say your companion is a court jester in your land? Then let him entertain me…we are in need of someone to amuse us."

"Now what'd ya get me into?" stammered Kyle.

Placing her hand over her mouth, Abby whispered, "Relax, if we can keep this king happy, then maybe he won't wanna get rid of us."

"Whatta ya suggest I do?" Kyle asked.

This time, it was Abby who laughed. It seemed to confuse not only the king, but Kyle as well.

"What's so funny?"

"Well," Abby responded, "I was thinking maybe ya could do some of your rap songs you always goof around with… ya know, make something up and jump around a little bit."

Glancing over at the king, Kyle could see that he was getting impatient. He knew it was now or never. The only question was would King Cyrus like it?

by Corbin P. , 11

The Ragamites

Leading me and Kate, Zeke continued on the same path. We both tried to be as quiet as possible, partly because we didn't want any more surprises, and partly because we were worried about Kyle and Abby.

Off in the distance, beyond a wide valley, we were finally able to see the walls of the Ragamite Village. Although the village was far away, it still seemed big. It extended between two mountain ranges that appeared to be many miles apart.

"Zeke!" I cried out. "Is that the Ragamite village?"

"Indeed it is. We need to travel through the Valley of Bones, and we'll be there."

Stopping in her tracks, Kate asked, "Did he say a valley of bones?"

Looking around for a stray skull or rib, I paused. "Yeah, that's exactly what he said."

"Why does that not surprise me?" Kate stared at my pants pocket. "Quick Parker, pull out the bottle, so we can see how many strings are still left."

"Why?" I demanded. "Something got ya spooked?"

"Well, seems to me if we're about to go through a valley of bones then we better be prepared to possibly lose a string."

"What? From a bunch, of dead skeletons?" I laughed.

Catching up to Zeke, Kate replied, "Who knows how they got that way and what else we might come across."

"What do ya think, Zeke?"

Grinning like a Cheshire cat, or should I say, Mancoon, he said, "Well…only one way to find out."

So, we set off through the Valley of Bones, hoping to arrive at the Ragamite village without any problems.

Walking through the valley was not as terrible as I thought it might be. There were lots and lots of bones all about us, but to me it was actually kinda cool. I felt a distinctive presence the entire time we ventured forward. Kate was clearly on the edge the entire time. She didn't feel a presence around us as I did. Actually all she did was walk fast and said remarkably little.

I decided to take the time and ask Zeke lots of questions. Like where did these bones come from? Who'd they belong too? Why are they still here?

Of course in typical Zeke fashion, all he would say was, "You will know soon enough."

Something in what Zeke said made me think I would be involved with the Valley of Bones somehow. Probably real soon.

Kate was the first to arrive at the village gate; as a matter of fact, Zeke and I had to hurry to catch up with her.

"You a little anxious, Kate?" I asked in a snicker.

"No, I just wanna meet the Ragamite people and get started on solving this problem."

I knew better. The bones plainly spooked her. We waited outside the gates wondering what we needed to do next. I kinda gave up asking Zeke questions, since he almost always answered like my mother. "You'll see."

Suddenly we heard a tremendous clatter coming from the other side of the wall. The sound of levers and gears grinding together suggested one thing. Immediately, the mammoth double doors opened. We had to rush quickly out of their path.

I then stared at the oddest-looking creature I had ever seen. It was made of rock like the watchman we met earlier in our journey. But this one was different in one special way. Standing twice as tall as us, with two stony arms, this

Ragamite also had three legs!

When it approached it moved by using one leg at a time. First the right leg, followed by the middle leg and then the left leg. As a result, it covered a lot of ground but at an extremely slow pace. Everything about this Ragamite was extremely slow.

It towered over us not making a sound. I felt as if it was waiting for us to make the next move. So I did. Grinning, I raised my hand in a friendly gesture. The Ragamite cocked his head to one side and abruptly turned away from us.

"What'd I do?"

"Nothing," Zeke replied. "Now we must wait."

"Wait for what?" Kate asked.

"As you can tell, everything about the Ragamites is done at a slow, controlled pace…"

"That's for sure," Kate interrupted.

"So in order for us to connect with them, we must be patient in all that we do."

Frustrated, Kate said, "But we don't have enough time to work slowly."

"Yeah, in case ya haven't noticed we're down to three strings," I added.

Zeke whirled around to face us. Something told me we were about to get another lecture.

"As I stated awhile back, time is no longer on our side."

"Zeke is this another one of your riddles?" I asked cautiously.

"Not at all, it's a test of patience…it's learning to do things on God's schedule and not your own."

Shrugging my shoulders, I remained silent. None of us felt like being patient, especially when we were faced with having to get something done as soon as possible.

Finally, the Ragamite moved forward into the fortress. Following him, we kept a safe distance. The inside of the village was massive, yet everything seemed a little primitive. They lived in huts made of stones with stick roofs. Even the tools they used looked as if they were hundreds of years old.

We must have been quite a sight to behold. Eyeing us were hundreds of curious Ragamites. They seemed to be gentle creatures. We were never threatened in any way.

As we continued to follow our guide, we saw an enormous structure off in the distance. It stood out among all the other buildings because it was the only one that had color. Reaching at least fifty feet upward, the golden object shimmered. But the shape was what actually made it appear odd. It looked like a giant triangle.

Gathered about the golden triangle were hundreds of

Ragamites. They stood before it, arms raised high.

"What is that?" I shouted.

"And what are they doing?" Kate added.

"That, young ones, is the reason you are here."

Kate and I took our eyes off the structure momentarily to glance at each other. Then we realized what the golden triangle was.

"That's the idol the Ragamites have been worshipping, isn't it?" Kate exclaimed.

"It's actually pretty neat looking." Staring at the object, I paid no attention to anything around me.

"Yeah, it is. It seems to point straight up to Heaven."

Zeke startled us with his next action. Transforming into a beautiful white stallion, he kicked up the dirt around us. Choking from the dust in the air, Kate and I stopped gawking at the idol.

"I suggest you two peel your eyes away from that idol and take a look at your bottle."

I swiftly pulled the bottle out. "Not again!" I shouted. "We've lost another string."

Sheepishly, Kate glanced over at Zeke. She knew he was disappointed.

"We were punished for that, weren't we?" Kate asked.

"Indeed you were. You two were acting no better than the Ragamites…one must realize that an idol is nothing more than an object or desire that takes the place of God!"

"You mean like money, or a car?"

"Or even someone famous." Kate added.

"Exactly," Zeke glanced at the idol one more time. "Remember, you are here to save the Ragamites."

I hung my head in shame. "Because of our foolish mistake we're now down to two strings." I meekly looked up at Zeke.

"What should we do now?" Kate asked.

"Each of you should humble yourselves before God… perhaps you will both then discover a unique gift."

Without saying another word or asking another question, Kate and I silently sought God's forgiveness. As I prayed to the Lord, I suddenly felt a sensation throughout my body. A sense of warmth engulfed me; a tremendous feeling of confidence seemed to take over, as well.

Kate experienced the same sensation.

Startled by the sound of a trumpet, we heard enthusiastic shouts erupting from the crowd. I looked over at Zeke hoping for an answer. "What's going on?"

"It is time to meet the king of the Ragamites."

It didn't take long for the villagers to quiet down. Each and every one of them bowed down before a creature much larger than themselves.

"I think we need to bow as well," I whispered to Kate.

Falling to my knees, I glanced over at Zeke. Even as a horse he was kneeling before the king. The king was regal looking. He wore a crown of gold and held a scepter made of granite. At the end of the scepter was an incredibly shiny stone. I figured it must have been a diamond.

"You may rise, visitors from unknown," he announced. "I am King Teman, and I welcome you to the village of Dedan."

Standing before the king I actually felt comfortable in his presence. There was something about him that seemed likable, although I wasn't sure why.

"King Teman," Zeke announced. "I am Ezekiel from the clan of the Tree Travelers. And these are two human children, Kate and Parker."

The smiling king looked Kate over. It was as if he knew her from somewhere. "You are the child who has been part of my dreams," the king announced, pointing at Kate.

"Really?" Kate asked.

"Perhaps you have been sent here by Bel, the god that the

Dolamites have commanded us to worship."

"Who's Bel?" I asked Zeke.

Zeke put a hoof up to his mouth in a silencing gesture.

Standing defiantly, Kate faced the king. She had fire in her eyes, and her fists were balled up. "You're mistaken! It may be true, that I have appeared in some of your dreams. But it's the God of all creation…the God you've forsaken, who has sent me."

All I could think was, *Oh no! Now she's done it. This king is going to wipe us out.* But, a remarkable thing happened. The king had the look of a small child on his face, a child who appeared confused. Then he became quite anxious and motioned for a couple of villagers.

"You three must come with me," the king commanded. "There is much I wish to discuss."

While being led through the village streets, I turned toward Kate. "Wow, what got into you?"

"I don't know," Kate shrugged her shoulders. "I guess I suddenly became angry at him for mentioning the idol he worships. After that, I realized what we must now do."

"What?" I asked. "What're we suppose to do?"

Kate looked embarrassed as she struggled with her answer. One moment she was spitting nails, and the next she was…humbled and embarrassed.

Turning to Zeke, I asked, "What does she mean?"

"Parker," Zeke exclaimed, "do you remember a while back when I told the four of you that you are all here for a specific reason?"

"Sure, ya said we all have a certain talent, and we'll find out what it is during this quest."

"Well," Zeke continued, "Kate is beginning realize what her talent is, and why God has chosen her to help the Ragamites."

"What is it?" I demanded.

Zeke remained silent. But Kate spoke up. "God wants me to interpret the king's dreams, doesn't He?"

"Yes He does," Zeke answered.

Zeke focused his attention on Kate as I listened, amazed by what was happening.

"Kate, you have the gift of prophecy and understanding…you are unique in that you are a great listener, yet you can be persuasive when you speak to others."

"But how will that stop the Ragamites from worshipping an idol?" I interjected.

Zeke remained silent for a moment, waiting for Kate to

think about the question.

"Because, if I can interpret the king's dream, I might be able to convince him to stop this sin and turn back to God."

"I'm glad it's your gift and not mine," I announced.

Almost as if on cue, Zeke and Kate both turned to look at me. I thought, *Uh no, what's next?*

"Your gift is also special." Rearing up on his two back legs, Zeke certainly got my attention. "You are a natural born leader…and your role will require this gift and more."

Just as I was about to ask Zeke another question, we arrived at what appeared to be the king's palace. I was suddenly overwhelmed by its sheer size. The palace was carved into a mountain and was entirely open. It looked out over the valley beyond. It had a huge terrace high above the village, with a balcony that overlooked the valley.

After gesturing for us to sit, the king's attendant's left the balcony area. But something told me we weren't here for tea and crumpets.

by Kate G. age 10

8

Turning toward Abby, Kyle frowned. Somehow he had to entertain the king of the Dolamites or the king might entertain the thought of getting rid of them.

What should I do? What should I do? he thought. All the while, King Cyrus seemed to be growing impatient. Then Kyle knelt down to one knee and bowed his head. Although it seemed as if he was paying tribute to the king, he was not. Closing his eyes, he silently began to pray to God.

Within a matter of moments, a sense of peace engulfed him. Kyle instantly smiled up at Abby. She had been silently praying as well. Abby grinned back at Kyle, and he knew what he needed to do.

Leaping to his feet, startling everyone around him, Kyle proclaimed, "In my land, King Cyrus, you would probably enjoy rock and roll music." Winking at Abby, he continued, "But I have a style I think you're gonna like even better...it's called rap."

Kyle motioned for Abby to play along with him. He started to dance and gesture with his hands. Abby cupped both her hands together. Placing them around her mouth, she began making rap noises for Kyle.

"Good King Cyrus," Kyle rapped, "was a merry old soul, and a ruler of strength was he. He controlled all the land, with his subjects at hand as far as the eye could see."

Kyle shrugged his shoulders and glanced over at Abby. Shrugging hers in response, she continued to make rapping sounds. The good news was that King Cyrus seemed to enjoy it all. He took his seat on the throne and bobbed his head back and forth to the song.

"Now there came a day, that he was said to say, I will conquer anyone in my path. So the king drew his army of stone together, and brought down his mighty wrath."

Swaying back and forth was the king getting into the song. Kyle started to giggle at the sight. He knew better than to look over at Abby, so he continued to rap.

"But the God of all creation said, 'Oh no king, ya mustn't attack yet. Ya must prepare yourselves for the coming battle and wait for another sunset.'"

Then King Cyrus waved his scepter. Shouting, he brought an immediate end to Kyle's song. "Stop! Stop this music!"

King Cyrus moved swiftly toward Kyle and Abby. Standing right in front of them, he demanded, "How? How did you know of my plans to attack the Ragamites? And why should I wait another day and not attack today?"

The king was clearly agitated, but also confused. Throughout his tirade, Kyle and Abby maintained their composure. They waited for King Cyrus to settle down.

Recognizing what just happened, Kyle was now clear on what their mission was. He and Abby were there to stall the Dolamites from attacking the Ragamites. The question was, would one more day be enough for Parker and Kate to convince the Ragamites to repent?

Seizing the opportunity, Abby announced, "We know of your brave plan, King Cyrus. But we also know that now is not the time to go forward with this plan."

King Cyrus looked first at Abby and then at Kyle like a puppy waiting for a command.

"That's right," Kyle added. "It would be disastrous if ya attacked today…surely your wisdom tells you that another day of preparation would be wise?"

Dropping his head down slightly, the king began to rub what appeared to be his chin. He was thinking intently about what Kyle and Abby said. A few seconds seemed like an eternity as they awaited his response.

"I will listen to your advice and wait an additional day. But tomorrow…the battle begins." Gesturing with his tiny hand, Cyrus added, "And you two will accompany me. You will witness our victory!"

All the Dolamites began to cheer and celebrate. The noise was deafening. There's nothing quite like the sound of rocks banging against rocks. Abby patted Kyle on his back, and he returned the gesture. They may have bought some extra time, but would it be enough?

***

Back in the Ragamite village, Parker and Kate looked out over what would probably be the battlefield between the Dolamites and Ragamites. And from what they could tell from this peaceful people, the Ragamites wouldn't stand a chance if they fought.

Pacing back and forth along the balcony, King Teman was obviously lost in deep thought. Something was troubling him. I figured it was the dreams he had.

"Hey Zeke," I whispered. "What's next? I mean…what does he want us to do?"

Zeke, in his typical fashion, replied, "You will soon find

out."

The king then motioned for us to stand. Standing directly in front of Kate, tilting his head to one side, he looked at her quizzically.

"I have had a dream. One that has perplexed me greatly." Pausing, the king then added, "No one has been able to interpret this dream…so I continue to have it." He pointed his stony finger at Kate. Kneeling down, so he could be at her eye level, King Teman bellowed, "You will tell me what this dream means!"

In a calm and collected manner, Kate put both of her hands on the king's shoulders. All of the king's attendants gasped. Without flinching, Kate looked him squarely in the eyes. "All you need to do is tell me this dream, and I will do my best to help you." Smiling affectionately, Kate removed her hands.

The king rose. He began to pace again, taking short deliberate steps. "Here is my dream; interpret it for me. Out in the great valley, the Valley of Bones, stood a tree…it was an enormous tree. It was a beautiful tree; one that reached up to the heavens with many branches and an abundance of fruit. Then out of the heavens, came a messenger, a holy one, who approached me with these words."

Staring out into the valley, King Teman said, "'This tree

will be cut down, and all its branches will wither away. Only its stump will remain, nothing else will survive. This is the word of the Most High, who is sovereign over all.'" King Teman glared at Kate. "Now, young one, you must tell me what this dream means."

Kate turned away from King Teman and looked out over the balcony into the valley below. She was extremely perplexed and took a few moments before she turned to face the king again. "King Teman, if only your dream didn't apply to you, but to your enemies…The tree you saw represents your kingdom. It has grown great and proud, and all its branches represent your subjects." Kate hesitated before continuing. "But, when the Holy One announced that the great tree must be cut down, He meant that you and your people will be destroyed. Only a small fragment of your civilization will be left. I'm afraid you and your subjects will be wiped out by the Dolamites!"

The king dropped to one knee, immensely saddened by Kate's interpretation.

"This cannot be!" he shouted. "How could my kingdom be annialated? How could all be lost?"

Approaching the king, Kate looked into his eyes. "It doesn't have to be this way. There's still time to repent and change your ways."

"I don't believe it," King Teman cried out defiantly. "This can't be right."

Taking a step back, Kate added, "Just stop your idol worshipping and denounce the god, Bel. Maybe all will be forgiven."

The bottle inside my pocket started to shake. I immediately withdrew it and knew what happened. Another string had disappeared…we were now down to one!

Returning to his feet, the king walked away. Kate turned and saw that I was holding the bottle by its last string. She rushed over to my side, and we stared at the bottle not saying a word.

Sensing our disappointment, Zeke finally broke the silence. "Take heart my friends, all is not lost, yet."

"What'd ya mean by yet?" I asked. Then it dawned on me what Kate had just done. Glancing at Kate, I said, "You know, what you did was amazing. You really did see his dreams, didn't you?"

Grinning, Kate took heart from what I said. "It was so clear…I mean the Lord's words were inside me. I guess all I could do was say them."

"I just hope you got through." I held the bottle up high. "Because we are down to one string."

"Ah," Zeke announced. "One more string means one more

chance."

"What'd ya mean, one more chance?" Kate asked.

Zeke gave us a wink and smiled. It was a gesture that indicated that it's not over yet. Of course, Kate and I weren't going to allow him to be silent this time.

"You know something, Zeke. And right now we need to hear it," Kate demanded.

"Yeah Zeke, don't leave us hanging."

"If this will help you to sleep better, then I guess I can spill the beans," Zeke laughed. "Tonight King Teman will see another sign. A sign he will not be able to understand, nor will anyone else. But, this will be his last chance."

I gazed at Kate. This was her area of expertise.

"In the morning he will seek your help again, Kate."

"To interpret this sign?" she interrupted.

"Exactly, but you will not be the only one who must step forward." Turning his attention toward me, Zeke continued. "You, Parker, will be called to do something quite extraordinary."

"What? What?" I shouted.

"You both will find out in the morning," Zeke countered. "But now you must both get your rest. Tomorrow will be a telling day."

9

During the night, neither Kate nor I were able to sleep well. I kept staring at the bottle that somehow still seemed to shimmer in the dark. We were down to one string, and the Ragamites were more than likely about to be destroyed. Everything seemed to hinge on convincing King Teman to repent of his sinful idol worshipping. But how?

I also kept wondering about Kyle and Abby. Were they all right? Would we see them soon? For that matter, what was their role in all this? But all these questions quickly went away as the day began to unfold in a dramatic way.

Bursting into my shelter, Kate couldn't contain her excitement. "Parker, Parker, come quick!"

She didn't give me much of a chance to respond. She turned and sped out of the room. Running after her as fast as I could go, I heard a thundering commotion outside the city gates. When I finally caught up to Kate, she was standing on the balcony next to Zeke. They stared off in the horizon.

Then it caught my eye. Clouds of dust could be seen far, far away. A low rumbling sound filled the air. Everything in me said this was not good.

"Zeke," I shouted. "What is that?"

"It's the Dolamites!" Kate shouted. "Zeke said their soldiers are heading this way."

"Good gracious! It's too late."

"What do we do?" Kate asked.

While staring at the dust cloud advancing toward us, Zeke had something remarkable happen. A sensational bolt of light engulfed him. Backing away, I shielded my eyes. In an instant, the radiance disappeared. There, standing before us was Zeke, in his true form. He was now a Tree Traveler, human in almost every way. He held in his unique suction cup hands one sword and one shield. And upon his head he wore a regal looking crown that shone with a dazzling display of brilliance. Zeke looked every bit a warrior, including his game face.

"Now, my friends you see me in my true form, that of a warrior prince ready for battle…for it will not be long before the Dolamites arrive and attack."

Instinctively the three of us fell to our knees and bowed our heads. There was only one thing left to do. Pray. After a few moments, we were interrupted by one of King Teman's guards. The king was summoning us.

When we arrived in the king's chambers, he was quite upset and sullen. Stepping forward, Zeke was the first to speak.

"King Teman, it is I, Ezekiel in my real form. How can we assist you?"

"My watchmen inform me the Dolamites are on the move." Focusing his eyes on Kate, he added, "You foresaw this young one…but I am still not convinced they come to do us harm."

"Surely you realize they are coming here to drive you out and destroy your people?" Zeke asked. "How much longer are you going to sit there and do nothing?"

Flashing anger toward Zeke, King Teman said, "Even if you are of noble birth and a prince in your land, it does not excuse you of speaking to me in that manner…I have a mind of setting you and your friends out there, and letting you deal with the Dolamites."

Feeling a little confused and frightened, Kate whispered to me. "What's Zeke trying to do?"

I thought for a moment and glanced over at the king, who was still fuming. Then I realized what Zeke was up to.

"He's trying to get King Teman mad enough to stand up for himself. I think he's trying to get him to see he can't win without God!"

A few more moments passed in silence. It was a stare down between Zeke and King Teman. Neither was ready to give in. Then the quiet was finally broken by the sounds of horns blaring. Quickly, we dashed toward the balcony and saw why.

The clouds of dust diminished. Scores of Ragamites ran for the safety of the village gates. A small scouting party of Dolamites was pursuing them. The petrified Ragamites were running for their lives.

"If you won't fight for your people, I will!" Zeke shouted. "And if you won't turn to God, then you will be destroyed…you have set your own dream in motion."

King Teman seemed to agonize over Zeke's last statement, but he still refused to do anything.

"Kate," Zeke announced, "you stay here with King Teman. God is not through using you. You have one more shot at convincing him." Placing both his hands on Kate's shoulders, Zeke said, "Trust in the Lord."

Then Zeke turned his attention toward me. "Parker, it is now your time."

Somewhat shocked, I said nothing.

"You will lead us in battle against the Dolamites."

"Whoa now," I answered. "What do ya mean *lead us in battle with the Dolamites*?"

"Do you remember when I said your test will come this morning?"

"Yeah!"

"Follow me down into the valley. And like Kate, trust in the Lord."

Turning towards Kate, I watched Zeke walk away. "So he thinks the two of us are gonna hold off these Dolamites, huh?" Not waiting for a response, I followed Zeke.

Kate shouted out to me as I was about to go down the stairs. "Parker, ya can do it…we both can do it. Have faith."

I held up the bottle in a show of agreement, realizing it was probably my only weapon. At least Zeke had a sword!

***

The Dolamite army continued to advance. King Cyrus sat back in his mobile throne watching from a safe distance. Sitting alongside him were Kyle and Abby. They watched in horror as the much stronger and larger soldiers marched toward the Ragamite village. There was nothing left for them to do but pray that Kate and Parker could somehow get through to the Ragamite King. From where they were sitting it did not look bright for the Ragamites.

***

Zeke and I reached the gates of the village and requested that we be let outside. The guards looked at us dumbfounded, knowing that we faced an insurmountable task. When we were a considerable distance from the village, Zeke stopped. We were in the middle of the Valley of Bones. He turned to glance at the village walls now off in the distance. Then he turned in the opposite direction to face the advancing Dolamites. They were still a distance away.

"Now what?" I asked, somewhat shaken.

Zeke looked at me with a big grin on his face and a sparkle in his eye.

"Now we buy Kate some time to get through to King Teman."

"How?" I demanded. "By fighting thousands of rock soldiers by ourselves?"

"Not at all," he laughed. "By you commanding an army to join us."

"What army?"

"Look around you, young one. What do you see?"

Turning in every direction I tried to figure out what he meant. But all I saw was a bunch of old, dried up bones scattered about. Nothing else.

"Other than the fact that we have a bunch of old bones lying around us, I see very little...how can we...?"

Then it dawned on me. Actually it hit me like a ton of bricks. Zeke was referring to the bones. Could it be the bones would be our army? I looked over at Zeke. He stood patiently waiting for me to finish my thought.

"It's the bones, isn't it? We're gonna command an army of bones to help us fight the Dolamites!"

"Not we, Parker. *You*."

"Me? Me alone?"

"It is you who has the gift of leadership. It is you whom God has chosen to lead us into battle. Now you must reach deep down inside yourself. With the power of the Holy Spirit, command the dry bones to come alive."

Closing my eyes, I tried to envision an army of soldiers for God. Warriors afraid of nothing; warriors fighting for the good of God. Then I did something that took me totally by surprise. I raised my arms toward Heaven, and felt the Holy Spirit take over my thoughts.

Shouting out into the valley, I commanded, "Dry bones; hear the word of the Lord! May the breath of the Lord fill you and may you come to life."

The ground started to shake violently. A deafening rattling sound surrounded us. There before our eyes, bone gathered to bone. Structure came into being. The form and shape of mighty soldiers stood before us. Each one held a sword and shield. There, for as far as the eye could see, stood an entire army of bone soldiers, waiting for my next command.

Then I looked beside me and noticed Zeke was no longer there. Standing in line with the bone army, he was now facing me. Zeke raised his sword up high. With a loud clatter, the soldiers raised their swords in unison.

Zeke winked supportively. He stood silent, waiting for me to speak.

"Army of God," I shouted, without even realizing. "Face your enemy…and attack!"

What happened next was utterly unbelievable! The bone soldiers quickly ascended upon the Dolamites with such swiftness and courage that the Dolamites hardly had a chance to react. Even though the Dolamites were much bigger and stronger, they couldn't keep up with the lightning speed of the skeletal warriors. The battle was on. Now it was up to Kate to do her part.

***

King Teman sent for Kate to join him. She stood on his balcony, gawking at the scene below. When she walked back into his chamber, the king seemed sad and confused. He continued to pace back and forth. Even his personal guards paced with him as Kate patiently waited for King Teman to acknowledge her.

"Please sit, sit young one." King Teman gestured toward a chair.

Taking a seat, Kate waited for King Teman to speak.

"I am troubled by yet another sign," he spoke. "One that none of my advisors can interpret."

Kate didn't reply immediately. She realized that this was her final chance. It was do or die for the Ragamites, and it was up to her to convince them.

"Maybe I can help," Kate suggested.

The king turned away from Kate and walked over towards one of the walls. On the wall was a written message. But it was partially blocked by his presence. Turning toward Kate, King Teman motioned for her to join him.

by Corbin P. age 11

Frightened by something, the king's stony knees started
to knock together. Finally, he spoke. "Early this morning
I was visited by a spirit. As I sat in my chair pondering
what to do next, a finger appeared from nowhere and began
writing on this wall before you. I became alarmed at this
sight and ran from the room."

Glancing at the wall, Kate was confused.

"I know it is a sign," he continued, "but I do not know
from whom. No one has been able to interpret it, not my
enchanters, not my astrologers...now, I call upon you."

Kate stared at the writing a second time, still not
understanding what she was looking at. Suddenly

they heard a thundering commotion outside the king's chambers. Rushing past the king's guards was a servant who fell to his knees before the king.

"King Teman, a great battle is being waged in the Valley of Bones."

"What battle?" King Teman demanded.

"The watchman and the young human boy have summoned up an army of warriors." Gesturing with his granite hands the servant continued, "A great army of bone soldiers is engaged in battle against the Dolamites."

Turning his attention toward Kate, King Teman asked, "Do you know about this?"

Kate hesitated for a moment and then replied. "My friends, along with the power of God, are trying to defend you and your people. Only you refuse to believe." Pointing a finger at the king, Kate added, "And you're running out of time."

The king paced back and forth. Indecision weighed heavily on his mind.

Focusing on the wall, Kate closed her eyes. She prayed for guidance, and one last chance to convince King Teman. Opening her eyes, Kate looked at the message a third time. Tears flowed down her cheeks. Kate sank to the floor and wept.

"Young one," King Teman reached down to comfort her. "Why is it you cry?"

Kate slowly rose to her feet. Facing King Teman, she answered. "All through this adventure my friends and I have faced so many obstacles." Wiping the streaks from her face, she added, "And all through we have remained faithful. Never once did we question why. And now I feel as if I have failed, because I still can't see."

Tilting his head to one side, King Teman remained speechless.

"Then there is you, King Teman!" Fired up, Kate continued, "You have so much. You have been so richly blessed by God." Shaking her head, Kate added, "Yet even when others try to help you, ya still refuse to humble yourself."

Glaring at the king with defiance, Kate balled up her hands into fists. "Where's your faith?" she demanded. "Why'd ya continue to worship your false god, and defy the one true God who loves you?"

Growing to the size of saucers, King Teman's eyes stared back at Kate. But it was not she whom the king looked at. Staring beyond Kate, the king saw the words on the wall change. Now the writing was clearly visible for all to see!

King Teman collapsed to his knees and fell face first to the ground. Spinning around, Kate looked at what King Teman saw. Behind her, the sound of sorrow echoed throughout the room. King Teman wept and raised his hands toward Heaven. Streams of tears flowed through the crevices of his face.

"Lord, oh Lord God, please forgive me! Please forgive me!" King Teman shouted.

The Way Home

10

Instantly the conflict in the valley ended. Dust filtered through the air where warrior once fought warrior. Now there were none. Zeke and I stood silently staring out onto what was once a raging battlefield.

Slowly, two figures appeared on the horizon making their way through the murkiness and the dust. Zeke turned toward me and smiled, then waved me on to greet the approaching figures. I didn't hesitate. I immediately knew who it was. When I reached them, I threw my arms around my friends. Kyle and Abby returned the gesture.

"Man! That was amazing...can ya believe that battle?" Kyle cried out.

I smiled as we waited for Zeke to join us.

"Is it over?" Abby asked. "Did we win?"

"I guess we need to ask Zeke," I replied.

Pointing at a figure he had never seen before, Kyle asked. "Zeke, is that you?"

"Yes, this is my true self…and yes it is over. King Teman has repented."

Joining us was a joyous and exuberant person. Kate rushed into our circle so quickly she literally knocked Kyle and Abby down. The three of them rolled on the ground laughing and screaming at the top of their lungs. "We did it! We did it!" they shouted.

Out of pure delight and not wanting to be left out, I dove into the pile and joined my friends.

"Come on, join us Zeke," Kate yelled out. "It's time to celebrate."

"Ah, it may be, but it is also time for the four of you to rejoin your classmates."

Standing, I said, "I almost forgot about 'em."

"I don't wanna leave," Kyle added. "At least…at least not yet."

Joining Zeke and me, Kyle, Kate and Abby stood as well. We all realized it was time to leave. We also realized there was one last thing to do.

"The bottle," Kate exclaimed. "What about the bottle?"

Reaching into my pocket, I pulled it out. Ten pairs of eyes stared at it. We were amazed by what we saw. There was not one string still attached, but all four.

"Open it!" Abby yelled out.

"Yeah, the message," Kyle added. "It's supposed to tell us how to get back."

"Is there really a message inside?" I asked Zeke.

Gesturing with his hand toward the bottle, Zeke gave me his classic sly smile.

"I know, I know. There's only one way to find out."

As I twisted the cork that sealed the bottle, a slight hissing sound came from inside. Gentle wisps of smoke whispered their way out of the bottle. Finally, I turned the bottle upside down and placed my hands underneath to catch the contents within. Nothing happened.

"Here!" Kyle shouted. "Let me try."

Kyle grabbed the bottle from my hand and shook it violently hoping to dislodge anything inside. But still, nothing happened. Simultaneously, we all turned toward Zeke.

"What're we doing wrong?" I asked.

"Why's nothing happening?" Kate added.

Zeke remained silent, causing our anticipation to grow. Then he reached for the bottle and gently held it in both his hands.

"The message you seek is not contained within the

object…but, it can be found within these words."

We all exclaimed at once. "HUH?"

"Ya told us at the beginning of this quest, that there'd be a message waiting for us if we succeeded!" Abby whined.

"Yeah," Kyle chimed. "What'd ya mean by words?"

Kate turned to face Kyle and Abby. I stood off to the side.

"I get it," she stated. "He means he'll tell us how to get back." Gesturing with her hands, Kate added, "In other words, Zeke is the messenger."

"That's correct," Zeke replied. "Now, are you all ready for the message?"

"Go for it." Kyle and I shouted in unison.

❧

You must look within yourselves.
To find the way,
And reflect on what you've learned,
Throughout this day.

❧

Throwing his hands up out of frustration, Kyle scowled. Kate immediately laid into him. "Kyle Wright, don't ya give up so soon. We've come too far and gone through too much to quit now."

The look on Kyle's face was priceless. He was thoroughly surprised by Kate's words. Then he did something I'd never seen before. Smiling, Kyle nodded in agreement.

"You're right!" he barked. "Let's solve this riddle and get back to our class."

I patted Kyle on the back, as Zeke stood as tight lipped as ever. Clearly, he was waiting for us to come up with the answer.

"All right, what's *look within yourself*?" Abby asked.

"Well, I think the real question is what'd we learned about ourselves," I offered.

"And how does what we learned help get us out of here?" Kate asked.

We all looked over at Zeke for confirmation. At least he smiled back.

"Let's start with Abby," I said. "What do ya think ya learned about yourself?"

"Well," Abby paused. "I guess, I can face any problem and succeed."

"Don't forget, you're a great encourager," Kyle

interrupted.

"What do ya mean?" I asked.

"Hey, if Abby hadn't encouraged me to sing to that king, he would have attacked the Ragamites a lot sooner."

"You sang to the king?" Kate asked in a fit of laughter.

"Actually he rapped. He was pretty good too," Abby replied.

"All right then, what does that tell ya about yourself, Kyle?" I asked.

"That's easy," Abby spoke up. "I have to admit it. Kyle has the gift of being an entertainer."

That statement actually made Zeke laugh. Now we knew we were on to something.

"Your turn," I said, facing Kate.

"I guess I'm a good listener," she replied.

"Oh, not a listener," I added. "You were able to convince King Teman to change. And ya didn't do it by just listening."

"By the way." Abby asked. "How'd ya convince him?"

Walking over, Zeke joined us in our circle. He still didn't say anything, but he seemed ready to.

"Actually I got really mad at him, partly because he was so stubborn…and partly because I couldn't interpret the message on his wall."

"What message?" Kyle asked.

"I'm still not sure I understand it. Even after I was able to see it along with everyone else."

"That's because King Teman had to hear the anger coming from you." Zeke finally spoke up.

That definitely got all our attention.

"What do ya mean?" Kate demanded.

"It's quite simple, God was angry at King Teman for his defiance. But He wasn't ready to dismiss their civilization yet."

With all eyes on Zeke, we waited for him to continue.

"Basically, Kate, God used you to get King Teman's attention."

"To wake him up?" Kate asked.

"Yes. When King Teman realized the sacrifice that you and Kyle were making, he finally saw the love that God has for him." Displaying his hands toward heaven, Zeke added, "Sometimes we think too much of ourselves, and we need others to show us the way."

"But what did the message say?" both Abby and Kyle shouted.

"It seemed like it was some sort of scripture…but I don't

remember it all," Kate replied.

Closing his eyes, Zeke quoted what was written on the wall. "Psalm 10:11. He says to himself, 'God has forgotten; he covers his face and never sees.'"

"I'm still not sure what that means. But King Teman sure did."

"Why, Kate? What did the king do?" I asked.

Tears welled up in Kate's eyes before she added. "He fell to the floor and wept…then he pleaded out loud to God for forgiveness."

"Wow!" Kyle bellowed. "I wish I'd seen that."

Turning toward Zeke, Kate asked, "Please, Zeke. What does that scripture mean?"

"It means when a proud person depends on himself rather than on God, it causes God's guiding influence to leave his life."

"So King Teman finally realized he needed to put all his trust in God, and give up everything else?" Kate asked.

"Like we all must," Zeke answered.

We all still had some serious soul searching to do after hearing that story. I almost didn't want to think of what I learned. But my friends didn't let me off easy.

"So," Kate asked, as she turned toward me. "What'd you

learn, Parker?"

"Allow me to answer that question," Zeke jumped in. "Parker learned that he is a natural born leader, and that with complete faith, anything is possible."

I nodded my head in agreement; there truly was nothing I could add.

"So I guess if we sum it all up," Abby spoke. "We can't only rely on ourselves, or each other."

"We've gotta rely on God as well," Kyle added.

"Excellent!" Zeke shouted, startling us all. "Allow me to give you a little clue to my message."

"Go for it," I shouted.

"What is it?" Abby begged.

"On the other side of those rocks you will find your reflection...the rest is up to you."

Well, it didn't take another invitation for us to respond. We dashed over to the rocks and peered at the other side. There, staring us in the face was a pool of crystal clear water. Not large, mind you; about the size of a kiddy pool.

"The water's our reflection," Kate shouted, as she peered into it.

"Then that's it," I replied. "I guess all we gotta do is jump in."

"On the count of three," Kyle barked out. "One, two, three!"

Diving in together, we sank to the bottom of what seemed like a pond. I quickly made my move toward the surface as the others followed. Slowing down, we all broke through the surface together.

Amazingly, we were back in Meramec Cavern, swimming along in Mirror River. Standing above us was a familiar face.

"What took you so long?" Mr. Giff asked as he skimmed a stone across the water.

The End

Thank you for reading **Quest for God's Hidden Creatures: The Concealed Caverns.** If you liked this book, please share about it with your friends on Facebook and Twitter!

Be sure to find Tom Bazow's Author Page on Facebook and Twitter to keep up with all his news!

Other Titles by Tom Bazow

Quest for God's Hidden Creatures: The Legacy of the Doors

Quest for God's Hidden Creatures: The Concealed Caverns

Gedden's Armor

These titles are available wherever books are sold online

as printed or eBooks

Find out more about these titles and Tom Bazow

at his website:

SupernaturalArmor.com

Watch for more youth, young adult and adult

Christian supernatural fiction coming soon!

About The Author

Tom Bazow is an accomplished Christian author with three published books to his credit and one manuscript in the works. His latest novel, "*Gedden's Armor*," falls into the supernatural suspense/Christian fiction genre. *Gedden* is a YA thriller, which has received several favorable critical reviews. Tom was inspired to write *Gedden's Armor* while taking a group of his students on a field trip to the mysterious St. Louis City Museum.

Previous works include a faith-based children's series called "*Quest for God's Hidden Creatures*."

Tom and his wife, Warrine, live in St. Louis with their two daughters, Hannah and Molly. Visit Tom's website at SupernaturalArmor.com.

www.ingramcontent.com/pod-product-compliance
Lightning Source LLC
Chambersburg PA
CBHW060637130626
46555CB00002B/849